D1109870

The Lost & Found House

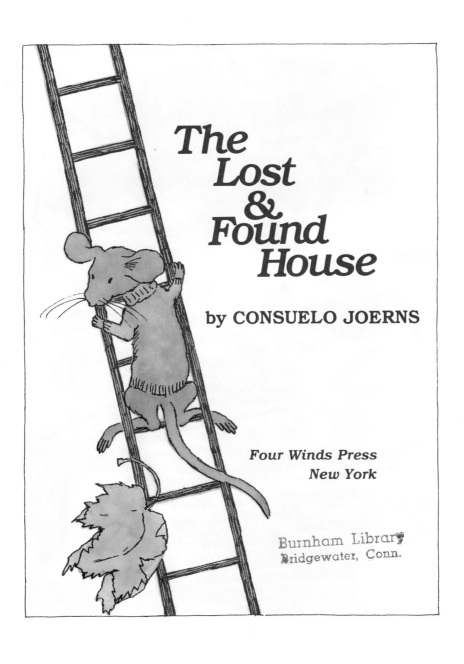

The Lost & Found House

by CONSUELO JOERNS

Four Winds Press
New York

LIBRARY OF CONGRESS CATALOGING IN PUBLICATION DATA
Joerns, Consuelo.
  The lost & found house.

  Summary: A mouse and his house suffer one mishap
after another until a boy with a model train takes
them in and provides a whole new life.
  [1. Mice — Fiction] I. Title.
  PZ7.J59Lo   [E]   79-11030
  ISBN 0-590-07627-2

PUBLISHED BY FOUR WINDS PRESS
A DIVISION OF SCHOLASTIC MAGAZINES, INC., NEW YORK, N.Y.
COPYRIGHT © 1979 BY CONSUELO JOERNS
ALL RIGHTS RESERVED
PRINTED IN THE UNITED STATES OF AMERICA
LIBRARY OF CONGRESS CATALOG CARD NUMBER: 79-11030
1 2 3 4 5 83 82 81 80 79

For Moth

When a sudden wind blew away his tree house,
Cricket had no place to live.

He looked everywhere for a new house. He found
a left-over bird's nest from last year, but it was too
small.

The dog house was too large — and had something
in it! Nothing he tried seemed right.

One day it rained and he ran for the old barn. It was dark and spooky, so he hid in a wheelbarrow till daybreak. When he woke up, he thought he must be dreaming —

there in the corner was a tiny house! It was slightly
falling apart, but it looked empty. His heart
thumped as he pushed the door. It creaked open.

Inside the house, the floor was covered with odds
and ends, and broken bits and pieces.

He went upstairs. There was nothing there but a
rickety bed and a mattress that needed stuffing.
The place was really a shambles.

Cricket set to work at once. He swept out the odds and ends with a broom.

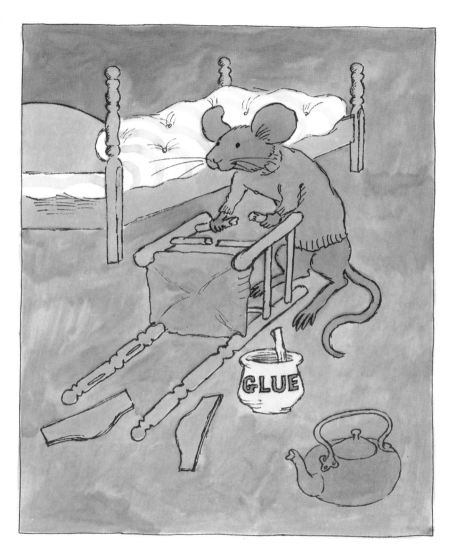

He glued the broken bits and pieces back together
again and stuffed the mattress full of soft hay.

He made new shingles for the roof and put up the
fallen shutters.

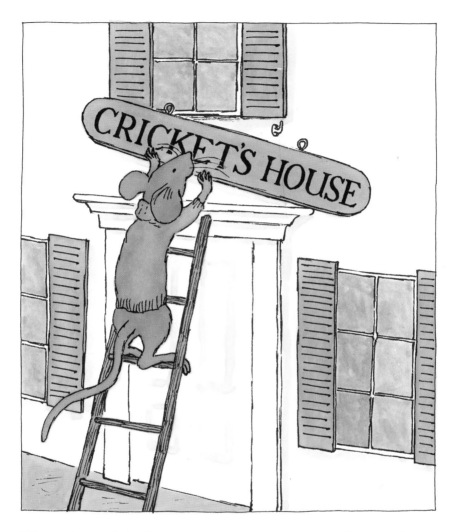

Then he painted CRICKET'S HOUSE on a sign and hung it over the door. At last Cricket moved into his new house, but. . .

the next day everything in the barn was taken out
and carted away to the dump.

Cricket had made the little house so handsome
that an antique dealer picked it up and put it in his
shop. That night Cricket went exploring. He found
a china bathtub and carried it home.

In the morning, a gentleman saw the house in the shop and wanted to buy it. He looked through the tiny windows at the furnishings inside.

Cricket heard him murmur: "X-squeeze-it! Purr-fec-shun!" and other such nonsense. The gentleman ordered the house to be crated and shipped.

The crate, marked FRAGILE, with the house inside
it and Cricket inside the house, was put on a ship
which sailed at midnight.

Not long after, there was a terrible storm. The ship hit some rocks and sank near the coast. The crate broke apart in the waves, but Cricket floated ashore on a wooden slat.

When the sun came up, he found his house washed
up on a sandy beach. Most of the furniture had
been swept out the door by the sea. Bit by bit,

it floated into shore. Cricket gathered the pieces on the beach and glued them back together again. Soon his house was as handsome as ever.

Then winter came and brought howling winds.
Shingles blew off the roof and let rain in through
the cracks.

Before Cricket could patch the roof, the rain
changed to snow. It snowed so much it blocked the
door and covered the windows, and still it kept on
snowing! It was dark inside and freezing cold.

After the snowstorm, a boy named Tom saw the
top of the house sticking out of a drift. He brushed
off the snow. "Just what I need — a station house
for my train!" said Tom with great excitement. He
carried the little house home.

Tom set the house down in his room. He was
about to take off the battered old sign and put up
one that said TOM'S STATION when he heard a tiny
cough. He looked in the window and saw

Cricket lying in bed, sniffling and sneezing. "Oh you poor mouse!" said Tom. He passed him a handkerchief through the window. "I thought the station house was empty!"

Cricket looked so miserable that Tom hardly knew what to do. He covered him with a mitten. He brought him some Very Special Soup. "When you get better," said Tom, "you can be my engineer and drive my train."

Cricket lay in bed for days snuggled under Tom's mitten, slowly getting better. He listened to the tap-tap-tap of Tom's hammer nailing down

shingles. In his sleep he heard the train roar past
his house, whistling. Then he had a fantastic dream
. . . but he woke up still in bed.

He ran to the window and looked out. The train
really was there, right in front of his house! Tom
had said he could drive the train, but where was
Tom? Cricket could not wait. He climbed into the
cab of the engine.

He found some knobs and switches, and a big lever that went back and forth. He leaned his paws on the lever and it swung forward. The train jumped ahead with a roar!

It raced along the tracks out of control. Soon his
house was far behind. The train thundered through
tunnels whistling. It whizzed over bridges. From
far away Cricket heard Tom's voice shout:

"Slow down!" But the more he leaned on the lever, the faster the train went. The whole world flew by in a blur. How would he ever find his house again? Now the train soared over a high trestle. He did not dare look out.

"Pull the lever BACK!" shouted Tom, this time
sounding nearer. At last Cricket understood what
to do. He clutched the lever and pulled it back as
far as it would go. The speeding train slowed down
and stopped.

Cricket tumbled out of the engine in a daze. He had stopped the train, but he had lost his house! Then he opened his eyes and —

there it was, settled beside the tracks with a
splendid new sign over the door. He had driven
Tom's train and stopped it to find his own
station house. At last he was home —
and he was Tom's engineer, too!

P   Joerns, Consuelo
J   The lost and found house

DATE DUE

JUL 1 0 1980	OCT. 1 4 1987		
SEP 1 1 1980	MAY 3 0 1992		
SEP 2 5 1980 JUN. 22 1987	JUN. 27 1992		
NOV 2 0 1980 JUL. 1 5 1987	JUL 2 2 1992		
JUN. 1 6 1982 NOV 1 1986	AUG 1 3 1992		
OCT. 2 8 1982 NOV. 2 8 1987	OCT. 1 5 1992		
JUN 3 0 1984 MAR 1 9 1988	FE 3 '96		
JUL 1 8 1985 AUG 1 1 1989	MAY 0 5 2010		
OCT. 1 0 1985 AUG 1 7 1989	OCT 1 6 2013		
OCT. 2 6 1985 AUG 2 9 1990	JUN 1 1 2015		
NOV. 3 0 1985 SEP. 1 2 1991			
OCT. 2 1986			

DEMCO 25-370